The Teeny Tiny Squirrel

written by
Jennifer Houp

illustrated by
Lauren Jones

For Mom & Dad.
Thank you for your support
during every adventure.
—JH

For Chloe & Carter.
May you always be kind and
curious. Love you always.
—LJ

Text copyright © 2017 by Jennifer Houp
Illustrations copyright © 2017 Lauren Jones
All rights reserved.
ISBN-13: 978-1546313106
ISBN-10: 1546313109

In a teeny tiny burrow,
in a big dark wood,
sat a teeny tiny squirrel
who was up to no good.

She had rummaged through the forest
and turned over every rock.

She'd collected every seed and nut

and stored them in her sock.

The forest floor was empty,

not a morsel left in sight.

But deep inside the burrow,

the food scattered left and right.

The teeny tiny squirrel lay down;

she'd stayed up half the night.

She quickly faded off to sleep

as twinkling stars shone bright.

When the sun came up that morning,

shouts of panic could be heard.

Not a tiny speck of food was found

for chipmunk, mouse, or bird.

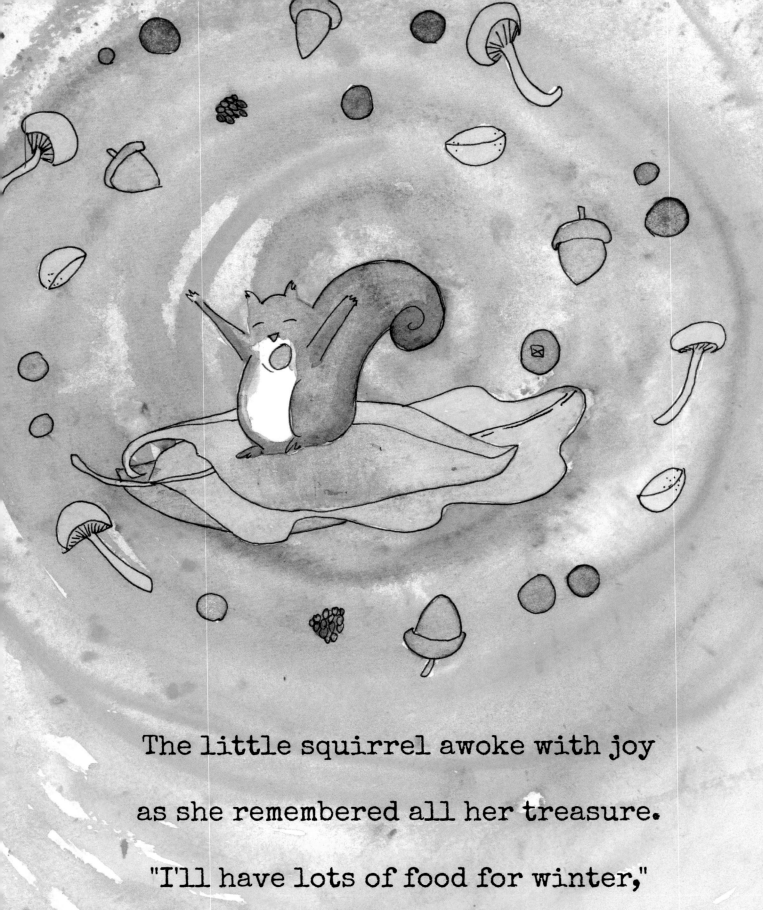

The little squirrel awoke with joy

as she remembered all her treasure.

"I'll have lots of food for winter,"

she shouted loudly with great pleasure!

But then she poked her tiny head
into the world around her.

Her friends were
running frantically.

(Except old salamander.)

"May I ask," she said
in a small hushed voice,
"whatever is the matter?"

"No food!" they cried,
as they scampered by,
with lots of noise
and clatter.

A sparrow landed on a branch,

head turning side to side.

"I cannot find a single seed!"

The tears fell as she cried.

A mouse ran by

with furrowed brow

and paused beneath a tree.

She softly muttered to herself,

"Is there something left for me?"

Just then a mommy chipmunk came

and sat upon a stone.

"How will I feed my baby

when I hear his hungry moan?"

The tiny squirrel sat gently down

and thought of what she'd done.

Instead of food for every mouth,

there'd be food for only one.

Her tiny heart
was very sad.

She knew she had
been greedy.

She'd gather all the food she took

and return it quick and speedy!

It took
all day

(and most
of night)

to put back
all the food,

but when she settled into bed,

her heart had felt renewed.

Her friends would have enough to eat

and so would little squirrel.

They'd share the forest's plunder

as the winter winds would swirl.

It doesn't matter what your size,

or if you're young or old.

We all can share the things we have,

from tiny seeds to gold.

The woodland creatures were so thankful that the teeny tiny squirrel put back all the food!

What are YOU thankful for?

When the squirrel decided to be generous instead of greedy, everyone had enough food for the long, cold winter!

What is something YOU could share with someone in need?

49728784R10018

Made in the USA
Middletown, DE
21 October 2017